This book is dedicated to my daughter, Nina Rose, and my mother, Gena Ann.

ISBN 13: 978-1-63489-116-5

Library of Congress Catalog Number: 2018933160

Printed in the United States of America

First Printing: 2018

22 21 20 19 18   1 2 3 4 5

Illustration and cover design by Stella Koh.
Interior design by Laura Mitchell.

Wise Ink Creative Publishing
837 Glenwood Avenue
Minneapolis, MN 55405
wiseinkpub.com

To order, visit www.itascabooks.com or call 1-800-901-3480. Reseller discounts available.

My Favorite Job Is You

By Ashley Flynn Illustrated by Stella Koh

I arise before you wake,
around the crack of dawn.
I make a cup of coffee
and get ready while I yawn.

When I hear you stirring,
I rush to see your face.
I missed you while we slept
And dreamt of your embrace.

It might sound kind of funny,
To miss you through the night.
But my time with you is short,
So every moment's a delight.

Our mornings are so hectic,
We try to be on time.
We change and feed and pack you up.
Sometimes we're in a bind!

It's very hard to leave you,
To say good-bye each day.
I often wonder if you'll be all right,
And if we'll both be okay.

Even though I'm at my job,
I think of you non-stop.
Clients, meetings, emails,
But your face is at the top.

My projects are important,
And I love the work I do.
I try my best to do well,
But my first concern is you.

It feels like a lifetime,
The time we spend apart.

But I remember you're a big girl,
Busy learning and growing smart.

The best part of my day
Is coming through that door.
Our eyes meet and you smile
As I sweep you off the floor.

Always so much to get done,

We have to pick and choose.

Errands, cleaning, laundry,

We have no time to lose!

It often seems unfair,
How fast the evening flies.
Sometimes I keep you up late
So we can play as a surprise.

Despite how full the day is,

We end it the same way.

I hold you close and rock you,

Whispering softly while we pray.

It can be a struggle,
This act of balancing.
I always feel so guilty,
Like I'm missing everything.

But as I hold you in my arms
And kiss your cheek goodnight,
I know God has a plan for us,
And it will all work out all right.

I may not know the future,
But I know this much is true.
You're my one and only,
And my favorite job is you!

Author Biography

Ashley's love for writing and poetry was ignited after the birth of her daughter. Nina Rose does not require much sleep, but requires much rocking. Many poems and story ideas flooded Ashley's tired mind while rocking her daughter to sleep. Ashley feels most inspired with her baby in her arms.

Before embarking on her new career as a children's book author, Ashley worked in the high-stakes world of political fundraising. Balancing a career she was passionate about with motherhood led Ashley to the idea of her first book, *My Favorite Job is You*. Ashley also has a deep love for ballet and teaches sweet two- to five-year-old ballerinas.

Ashley and her husband, Colby, have a precious daughter and an under-achieving (but luckily adorable) dog, Stewart. They live in Sioux Falls, South Dakota.